SHOWDOWN AT LONESOME PELLET

By Paul Rátz de Tagyos

Clarion Books/*New York*

Same coney, more lettuce.

Clarion Books
a Houghton Mifflin Company imprint
215 Park Avenue South, New York, NY 10003
Text and illustrations copyright © 1994 by Paul Rátz de Tagyos
The illustrations for this book were executed in marker on 100% rag marker paper.
The text was set in 14/18 pt. Garamond Book.

Printed in the USA

Library of Congress Cataloging-in-Publication Data

Rátz de Tagyos, Paul.
     Showdown at Lonesome Pellet / by Paul Rátz de Tagyos.
          p.   cm.
     Summary: Saladin, an unassuming hero who wears a radish hat, rescues
the Western coney town of Lonesome Pellet from the obnoxious Pointy Brothers.
     ISBN 0-395-67645-2
     [1. West (U.S.)—Fiction. 2. Rabbits—Fiction.]   I. Title.
     PZ7.R19395Sh   1994
     [E]—dc20   93-25733
                                                                       CIP
                                                                       AC

HOR   10   9   8   7   6   5   4   3   2   1

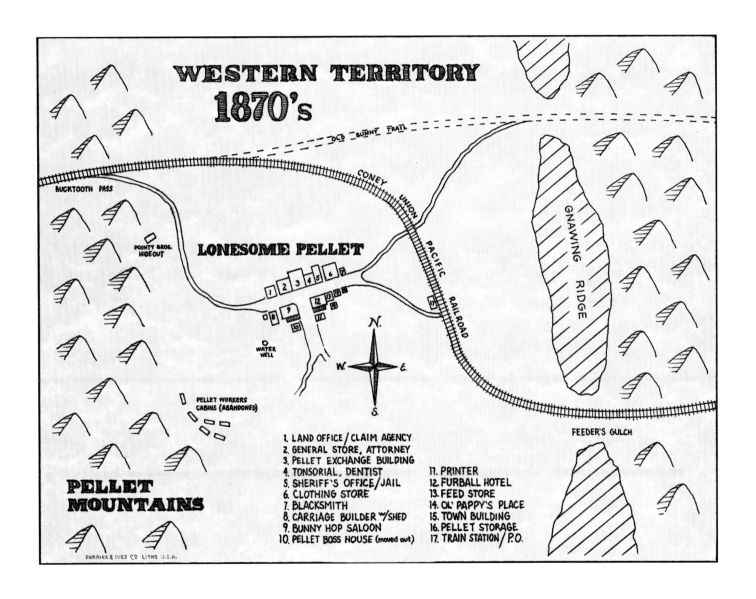

WESTERN TERRITORY
1870's

OLD BUNNY TRAIL

BUCKTOOTH PASS

CONEY UNION PACIFIC RAILROAD

POINTY BROS. HIDEOUT

LONESOME PELLET

GNAWING RIDGE

WATER WELL

N.
W. E.
S.

PELLET WORKERS CABINS (ABANDONED)

FEEDER'S GULCH

PELLET MOUNTAINS

1. LAND OFFICE / CLAIM AGENCY
2. GENERAL STORE, ATTORNEY
3. PELLET EXCHANGE BUILDING
4. TONSORIAL, DENTIST
5. SHERIFF'S OFFICE / JAIL
6. CLOTHING STORE
7. BLACKSMITH
8. CARRIAGE BUILDER w/ SHED
9. BUNNY HOP SALOON
10. PELLET BOSS HOUSE (moved out)
11. PRINTER
12. FURBALL HOTEL
13. FEED STORE
14. OL' PAPPY'S PLACE
15. TOWN BUILDING
16. PELLET STORAGE
17. TRAIN STATION / P.O.

FURRIER & IVES CO. LITHO U.S.A.

The Old West is full of legends, and the dusty little town of Lonesome Pellet can claim one. Back in the Pellet Rush days, it was a booming town. But those days had faded. Lonesome Pellet had become just another quiet little Western coney town.

Well, it used to be quiet—until the Pointy Brothers hopped into town. The Pointy Brothers were the meanest, orneriest coney coots that ever hopped the plains. All the townsfolk had heard that a stranger was going to come out of nowhere and save them, but nobody believed the rumor.

"These folks been hearin' too many stories about the Cone Ranger," said Clem. "He ain't real."

"No one's gonna take on the Pointy Brothers," said Ol' Pappy.

One morning, as the sun came up over the ridge, something else was coming up over the ridge as well: a stranger, wearing a radish hat—the likes of which had never been seen. He hopped into town and headed for the hotel.

He stared the desk clerk in the eye and rang the bell. *Ding. Ding. Ding. Ding. Ding. Ding. Ding. Ding.* "Nice bell," said the stranger.

"I reckon," said the clerk. "Nice hat."

"I'd like a room."

"First door upstairs on the left," said the clerk.

"Thank you kindly," said the stranger, tipping his radish hat and reaching for the bell. The clerk snatched it away just in time.

The stranger headed over to the sheriff's office.

"Howdy. Nice town," he said.

"Nice hat," said the sheriff.

"I hear you're having some trouble," said the stranger.

"No, we ain't got trouble," said the sheriff. "We got the Pointy Brothers, and they're worse than trouble. This town ain't had a moment's peace since they showed up."

"What do they do?" asked the stranger.

"Do? *Do?*" raged the sheriff. "They push good coneys around. They call coneys bad names. They steal feed and pellets. They even litter. What *don't* they do?"

"Well, you can rest easy now," said the stranger. He handed the sheriff a card that read:

SALADIN

HAVE FUR ~ WILL TRAVEL

"Saladin, eh?" said the sheriff. "I reckon you come from salad country."

"Yup, an' I'm gonna clean up Lonesome Pellet," said Saladin. "I'll have the Pointy Brothers outta here in three days' time."

"Why, that's impossible!" said the sheriff. "They're the meanest, orneriest, nastiest bunch of no-good coney coots I ever did see."

"Well, I'll get rid of 'em anyway," said Saladin. "I might need a little help from you, though."

"It's a deal," said the sheriff, and they shook paws.

That night, leaving his prized radish hat behind, Saladin paid a visit to the Bunny Hop Saloon.

He was standing at the bar with a glass of carrot juice when in hopped Eli
Pointy, the runt of the litter.

"Well, what have we here?" jeered Eli. "Stranger in town? Bought me a drink, I see." He snatched Saladin's glass and drained it in one gulp.

"Thanks, pal. . . . I said 'Thanks.' You're supposed to say 'You're welcome.'" But Saladin said nothing.

"Won't talk, eh?" said Eli. "Bartender, gimme a carrot juice." He poured the juice over Saladin's head.

All coney eyes were on Saladin as he turned and left the saloon without a word, carrot juice dripping from his ears. "Scared to fight, eh?" gloated Eli, laughing so hard he almost fell over.

By the next morning every coney in Lonesome Pellet had heard about the mysterious stranger.

"He's gonna clean up this town," said Clem.

"Naw, he ain't," said Ol' Pappy. "He's just as scared as we are. I'll bet he's already left town."

But that very night, Saladin was back in the Bunny Hop Saloon, this time wearing his amazing radish hat, when Eli Pointy hopped in. Everyone's fur went up a little.

"Nice hat," Eli said to Saladin. "Oh, and thanks for the drink." He grabbed Saladin's glass of carrot juice. "You know what?" he said. "The one thing that would pretty up this here hat is . . . some carrot juice!" He poured the juice over Saladin *and* his hat, laughing fit to bust. Saladin got up slowly and turned toward the door.

Suddenly he grabbed his rope and lassoed Eli, before Eli knew what hit him. The townsfolk gasped.

"Git this dern rope offa me, you varmint!" Eli demanded.

Saladin calmly ordered another juice, took a sip, and—*splat!*—threw the rest in Eli's face.

"Argh!" screamed Eli. "You made a big mistake, stranger. Me and my brothers will make you sorry. Just you wait till tomorrow!" And he hobbled out of the saloon.

"Hoo-wee!" said Clem. "Did you see that?"

"This stranger sure is fast on his hoppers," said Ol' Pappy.

Everyone wanted to buy Saladin a drink, but he refused politely and left the saloon.

Saladin returned to the hotel, pausing at the desk to ring the bell: *Ding. Ding. Ding. Ding. Ding. Ding. Ding. Ding. Ding. Ding. Ding. Ding. Ding. Ding. Ding. Ding. Ding.*

The startled clerk hopped to his feet as Saladin said, "Nice bell."

Meanwhile, back at the ranch, Eli told his brothers what had happened.

"Radish hat?" screamed Frank. "You let someone wearin' a radish hat do that to you?"

"I didn't see it comin'," whimpered Eli.

"Don't worry, little brother," said Jesse. "We'll teach him a lesson. Nobody does that to a Pointy Brother and gets away with it."

The next morning, anxious townsfolk gathered to see the showdown. Into town hopped the Pointy Brothers, a mighty mean-lookin' trio. Saladin was waiting for them, wearing his radish hat, another trusty rope by his side.

"You're gonna wish you was never furry," hollered Jesse.

"Yeah, we'll make weasel meal out of you," added Frank.

"I told you you'd be sorry," said Eli.

Saladin said nothing.

"What's the matter?" yelled Jesse. "Scared to fight?"

"Now, wait a minute," said Saladin. "I came here to make peace, not to fight."

"Too late," yelled the Pointy Brothers.

"But I've got a gift for you," said Saladin. "Looky here." He pulled out a strange-looking cart with a huge basket of fresh carrots in the middle. "These are for you. Take 'em, and there'll be no fighting."

"Heck, we'll take 'em and then we'll fight," yelled Jesse.

The Pointy Brothers moved toward the cart, eyeing it suspiciously.

"What's the matter? Scared of a few carrots?" asked Saladin.

"We ain't scared of nothin'," said Eli.

"Well, you sure look scared to me," said Saladin. "Look, folks. The big bad Pointy Brothers are scaredy-cats!"

Some coneys started giggling.

"We'll show you we ain't scared," blustered Frank, and the Pointy Brothers dove at the basket. Instantly Saladin's rope whistled through the air—*crack!*—and whipped away the stick that held up the top of the cart.

The top slammed down, capturing the three Pointy Brothers. "Climb aboard, folks," called Saladin. "Let's make sure these varmints don't get away."

With a crowd of coneys riding on top to hold down the lid, Saladin pulled the cart through the main street of Lonesome Pellet. They reached the railroad station just as the 12:20 train was pullin' in. Federal marshals were there to take the Pointy Brothers away for a long, long time.

The sheriff thanked Saladin on behalf of the whole town. In return, Saladin thanked the sheriff for helping him build the cart. "You did all the tough stuff," said the sheriff. "Life around here's gonna be a whole lot better without them mean, nasty, ornery Pointy Brothers. I wish there was some way we could repay you."

Saladin just looked over toward the Pellet Exchange Building.

For the rest of the day, Saladin
rang the big Pellet Exchange bell.
He rang it, and rang it, and rang it.

"That Saladin's quite a feller," said Clem.

"I'll say," said Ol' Pappy.

"He's a fine coney, all right," said the sheriff,
"but he sure puts the strange in stranger."

The desk clerk just nodded and said, "Nice bell."

Wouldn't you know it, right at sunset Saladin bade Lonesome Pellet farewell and hopped out of town, the radish hat sinking slowly in the west. And every day at high noon, they ring the tower bell in Lonesome Pellet to remember the town's greatest hero, Saladin—the radish hat that won the Coney West.